THE USBORNE BOOK OF AIR TRAVEL GAMES

Moira Butterfield

Edited by Tony Potter

Designed by Kim Blundell
and Nerissa Davies

Illustrated by Kim Blundell,
Chris Lyon and Guy Smith

Contents

About this book

There are lots of games, puzzles and activities in this book to play on plane trips or at home. Some can be played on your own, others in teams.

Games for more than one person are marked with the symbol above.

Long games are marked with this clock symbol. Save these until you have plenty of time to play them.

Fly with Mugsair

Below are the crew and passengers of Mugsair Airlines flight 321. They are about to fly from Fogsville airport to a holiday resort called Costa Fortune. You will meet them again on their journey in some of the games and puzzles in this book.

Crews are made up of cabin attendants and flight crew, such as the Captain, First Officer and Engineer. On a long flight you could ask an attendant if you can meet the Captain. On a short journey the flight crew will probably be too busy to meet passengers.

CREW

Flight attendant Ivor Tray

Flight Engineer Wil Itfly

James Pond

Rick Ord

1st. Officer Lou Smyway

Flight attendant Donna Panic

Captain Slog

Mrs Flight

PASSENGERS

Birdman Jack

Mr D. Racula

Lady Moneybags

Lotta Trouble

Ian Trouble

Mrs Bagsfull & baby

Peter Perfect

2

Captain's hat

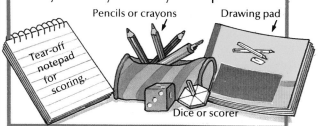

Lots of the puzzles in this book are marked with a picture of a Captain's hat like the one above. Each hat has a number marked on it. If you answer one of these puzzles correctly you can score the points shown on the hat. Keep a note of your scores and add them up when you have done all the Captain's hat puzzles in the book.

You could get up to 55 points. If you score over 40 points you qualify as an:

AIR TRAVEL GAMES CAPTAIN

Things you can take

You need to take the things below to be able to play some of the games in this book. It is a good idea to pack them in one small bag.

If you would like to keep a record of your flight there is a Captain's log to make on page 29. You need to get this ready before you start your trip.

Pencils or crayons • Drawing pad

Tear-off notepad for scoring.

Dice or scorer

How to make a scorer

If you don't have a dice you can make a scorer to use instead. You need a piece of stiff plain paper, some tracing paper, scissors, a pencil and a used wooden match or something similar.

1

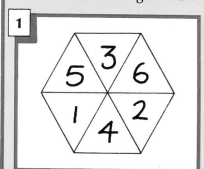

Trace the shape and lines above onto tracing paper, as carefully as you can.

2

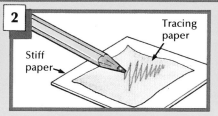

Tracing paper • Stiff paper

Put the tracing paper on top of the stiff paper, with the pencil marks face-downwards. Draw over them with a pencil to transfer the scorer shape to the stiff paper.

3

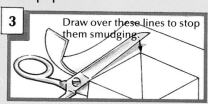

Draw over these lines to stop them smudging.

Carefully cut out the shape and mark one side with the numbers as shown in step 1.

4

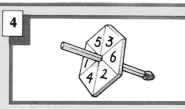

Push the match through the middle of the shape as shown above. You might find this easier to do if you first make a small hole with a scissor point.

5

A score of four.

Spin the scorer round on a table, like a top. You score the number shown on the edge which comes to rest.

Answers to all the puzzles in this book are on pages 30-32.

Camera clues

The Mugsair passengers are lining up to board their plane. A security guard is watching them on a video screen, but his camera is faulty and it has changed the picture. See if you can spot at least ten differences between the camera picture and the real scene.

VIDEO SCREEN

Let us out!

The Mugsair crew and flight attendants have accidentally been locked in the crew rest lounge. The key is in the wrong side of the door. See if you can work out how they get the key, using only the objects in the room.

The key is on the wrong side of this door.

Flight Engineer

1st. Officer

Captain

Whose jacket?

Airline flight crews have stripes on their jacket sleeves to show what job they do. The different stripes are shown below. The three members of the Mugsair flight crew locked in the lounge on the left have put on the wrong jackets. See if you can work out who's wearing whose.

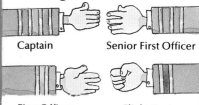

Captain   Senior First Officer

First Officer   Flight Engineer

Quick Games

Here are some quick games to try while lining up or waiting at the airport.

See how many direction signs you can spot to different parts of the airport. You could challenge someone else to see who can make the longest list.

See how many different jobs you can spot people doing at the airport. There is often a different kind of uniform for each kind of job. You could challenge a friend to see who spots the most.

Airport departure boards show the town or city, but not the country, where departing airplanes are flying to. Look at a departure board and see how many places you recognise. See if you can guess from the cities shown on the board below which countries the planes are going to visit.

Flight	Destination
323	Venice
297	Athens
345	Cairo
595	Moscow

Smuggler search

The escaped smuggler Hans Cuffed is shown below on a wanted poster.

WANTED

Hans Cuffed

Honor Plane

Abe Oveground

Ian Flightmovie

Ed Intheclouds

Dick Lare, the Fogsville Customs Officer, has stopped four passengers. Their passport photos are on the right. One of them is Hans Cuffed in disguise, using a false name. Who do you think Dick should arrest as the smuggler?

Dick Lare

In disguise

See how many ways you can disguise yourself by copying your passport photo* several times in a drawing pad, then adding different disguises to each drawing. There are some examples of disguises below.

Passport pieces

Some of the picture parts on the right are from Lady Moneybag's passport photo below. See if you can work out which ones don't fit.

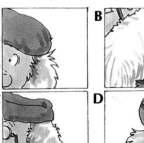

Lady Moneybags

A   B

C   D

E   F

*You could use an ordinary photo if you don't have a passport.

Anything to declare?

Air passengers arriving from abroad have to pay a tax, called "duty", for bringing some goods into the country. The Fogsville Customs Officers fine people if they find out that they have the goods but have not admitted it. In this game for three or more players everyone has a go at being a Customs Officer. Duty is paid in splots at Fogsville.

A splot ➤

Things you need

Before you start you need to make ten "sales slips" by copying the pictures and words on the right onto small pieces of paper. Put all the finished slips into a bag. Each slip shows an item and an amount of duty.

Sales slips for you to make.

Slip bag

Pair of earrings — 2 splots duty
Bottle of whiskey — 3 splots duty
Perfume — 4 splots duty
Radio — 5 splots duty
Watch — 6 splots duty
Camera — 8 splots duty
Diamond Ring — 12 splots duty
Fur coat — 13 splots duty
Necklace — 15 splots duty
Diamond tiara — 20 splots duty

How to play

1 One player starts off as the Customs Officer, the others as passengers. One passenger starts by picking out three sales slips from the bag with their eyes closed.

2 Add up the duty, and tell the Officer how much you owe. If your duty adds up to more than 25 splots, pretend you have less, like the player below.

I OWE 15 SPLOTS!

His duty adds up to 30 splots really.

3 The Officer can demand to see the slips you picked out if he thinks you are bluffing about your total. If you have bluffed the Customs Officer scores ten points.

Good Challenge. Score 10 Points

4 The Officer loses five points if his challenge is wrong. He must keep a note of how many points he scores. After your go put the slip back in the bag for the next player.

Wrong Challenge. Lose 5 Points

5 Each passenger gets two turns at picking out slips in a round. Choose a new Customs Officer from among the players after each round, until everyone has had a turn.

6 The winner is the player who scores most points during their turn as Customs Officer. You could end up with less than zero if you make too many wrong challenges.

7

Potty's planes

Here are five aircraft built by Mugsair's mad inventor, Professor Potty. Which is the odd one out?

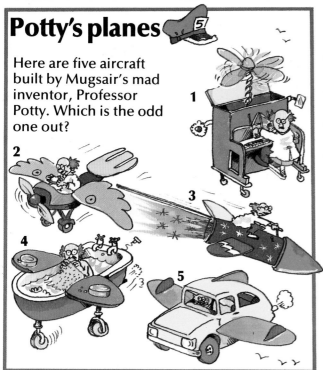

Sneaky spies

Top secret agent James Pond is one of the Mugsair passengers. He wants to get on the flight to Costa Fortune without being spotted by any enemy spies. Which way should he go through Fogsville airport to get to the plane without meeting any of them?

A spy looks like this

Entrance

James Pond

Air badges

Airline companies have their own badges. Look at the three pairs below to see if you can work out which of those in the box on the right makes up the fourth pair.

Aer Lingus (Ireland)	Air Canada
Pan Am (USA)	TWA (USA)

Qantas (Australia)	Icelandair
Lufthansa (W. Germany)	

Gulf Air (Gulf States)

Swissair

Olympic (Greece)

Did you know?

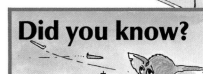

The King Khalid International airport in Saudi Arabia is the largest in the world. It covers 221 sq. km (86 sq. miles), the size of 27,532 international football fields. It also has the world's largest control tower.

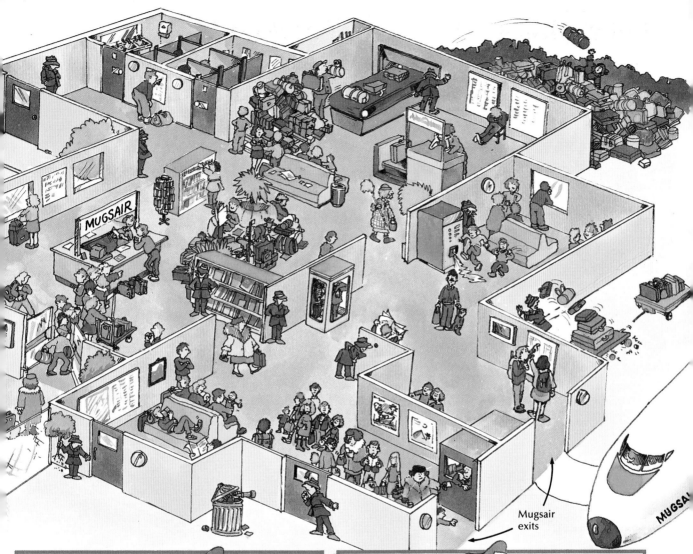

Mugsair exits

Spy catching

Five enemy spies follow James Pond onto the Mugsair flight. They are all hiding on the following pages in this book. See if you can spot all of them as you go through.

Who is it?

Birdman Jack is on the Mugsair trip because he is going on vacation with a relative in Costa Fortune: his mother's sister's father's wife. Who is he going to stay with?

Spot the planes

Lotta Trouble, Ian Trouble and Peter Perfect are plane spotting at Fogsville Airport, shown below. They have each made a list of the planes they can see, but only one is correct. Use the spotting guide on the right to work out which is the correct list.

Lotta
Boeing 747
DC9
DC10
Airbus

Ian
DC9
Boeing 747
Boeing 727
DC10

Peter
DC9
Airbus
Boeing 727
Boeing 747

Spotting guide

This spotting guide shows five popular planes, with some suggestions on things to look for to identify each aircraft. Four of them are parked at Fogsville airport below. You could use this guide to spot planes at your own airport.

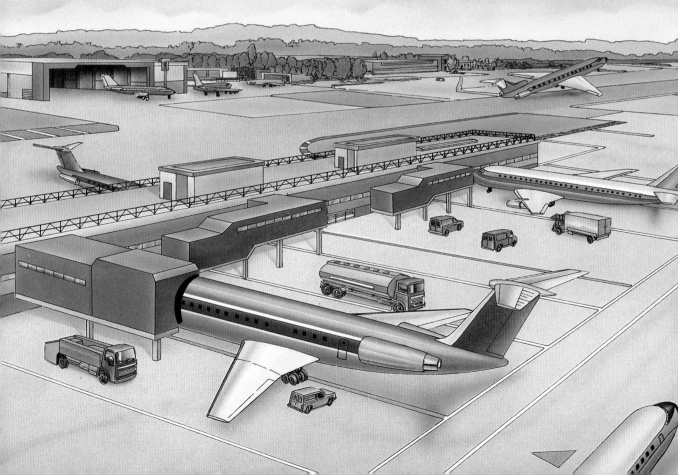

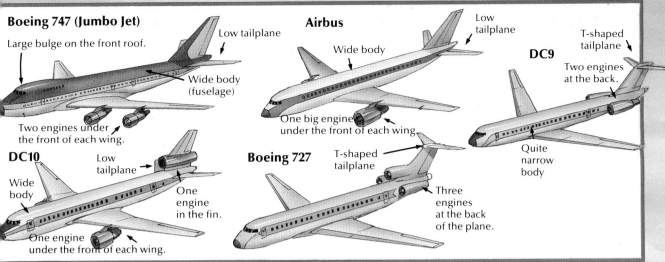

Boeing 747 (Jumbo Jet)

Large bulge on the front roof.

Low tailplane

Wide body (fuselage)

Two engines under the front of each wing.

Airbus

Wide body

Low tailplane

One big engine under the front of each wing.

DC9

T-shaped tailplane

Two engines at the back.

Quite narrow body

DC10

Wide body

Low tailplane

One engine in the fin.

One engine under the front of each wing.

Boeing 727

T-shaped tailplane

Three engines at the back of the plane.

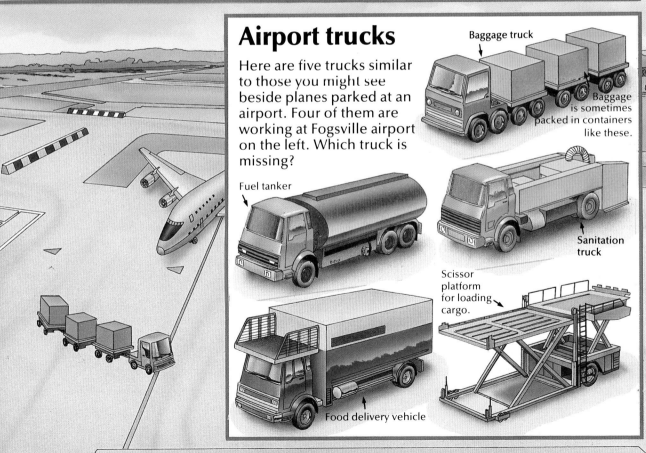

Airport trucks

Here are five trucks similar to those you might see beside planes parked at an airport. Four of them are working at Fogsville airport on the left. Which truck is missing?

Baggage truck

Baggage is sometimes packed in containers like these.

Fuel tanker

Sanitation truck

Scissor platform for loading cargo.

Food delivery vehicle

Seating plan

Six Mugsair passengers are about to sit in a block of seats. See if you can work out who sits in which seat from the clues below.

James Pond sits behind Lady Moneybags.

Lady Moneybags sits by a window.

Rick Ord sits two seats along from James Pond.

Lotta Trouble sits between two people.

Peter Perfect sits next to Lady Moneybags.

Mrs Bagsfull sits in the remaining seat.

A parking problem

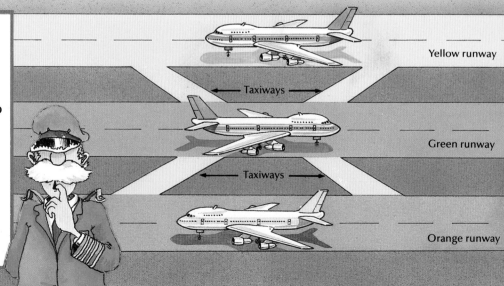

Three differently colored planes are on the wrong runways at Fogsville. Work out the best way to move them along the connecting paths (called taxiways) to their own runways, without allowing them to meet or park on the same runway together.

Yellow runway

Taxiways

Green runway

Taxiways

Orange runway

Truck mechanic

Hans Greasy, the Mugsair mechanic, has one hour to mend one of the trucks below. It takes him ten minutes to get some spark plugs from the store, and five minutes to find a wrench to fit wheel nuts. Which truck has he got time to mend?.

A Change plugs - 20 minutes

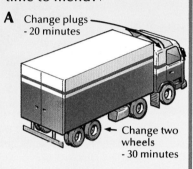

Change two wheels - 30 minutes

B Change plugs - 20 minutes

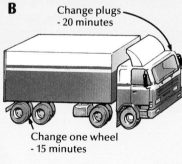

Change one wheel - 15 minutes

C

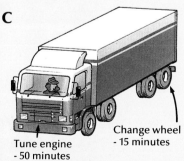

Tune engine - 50 minutes

Change wheel - 15 minutes

The take-off race

This is a race to see who can load all the cargo onto their plane first and then take-off.

Take turns to throw a dice or spin a scorer. Look at the boxes below to see what cargo you can load for each number you score.

You have to throw some numbers more than once to finish the game.

You need to get two luggage containers, three cargo containers and so on.

Once you have loaded all the items shown in the boxes you must throw a six to take-off. The player who takes off first wins the game. It is a good idea to keep a list of items as you load them, as shown below.

MRS BAGSFULL'S LIST
Film	I
Baggage	I
Cargo	II
Fuel	I
Food	II

In-flight film

Throw a 1
Collect 1 of these.

Baggage box

Throw a 2
Collect 2 of these.

Cargo container
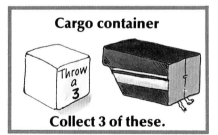
Throw a 3
Collect 3 of these.

Fuel load

Throw a 4
Collect 4 of these.

Food tray

Throw a 5
Collect 5 of these.

Throw a **6** to take-off

THE GREAT AIR QUIZ

There are three possible answers to each question in this quiz. Write down the question number, then the letter of the answer you think is correct. If you don't know the right answer try making a good guess. You can check to see how many you got right by looking at page 31. You could also try this quiz with a group of friends. Read out the questions and keep a note of who answers correctly. The person with the highest score is the winner.

1 Who was Orville Wright?

a The tallest ever pilot.
b The pilot of the first plane.
c The first world baggage-handling champion.

2 Who was Louis Bleriot?

a The first ever flight attendant.
b A famous airline chef.
c The first person to fly across the English Channel.

3 What is a Zeppelin?

a An airship.
b A German sausage sandwich invented by Louis Bleriot.
c The round bit in a plane engine.

4 What is an aileron?

a An air travel sickness pill.
b The square bit in a plane engine.
c An aircraft wing flap.

5 What is an airbridge?

a A game of cards.
b A tightrope between two airplanes.
c A passage which links a plane to an airport terminal.

6 What is a biplane?

a A stripy airplane.
b An airplane with double wings.
c A computerized airplane.

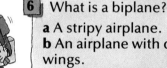

7 Where is Orly airport?

a Fogsville.
b The Bahamas.
c Paris.

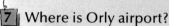

8 What is the Chicago O'Hare airport famous for?

a It sells the biggest hamburgers in the world.
b It is the busiest airport in the world.
c It was built in 1895.

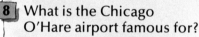

9 What do aircraft builders use a wind tunnel for?

a Working out a plane's shape.
b Cleaning a plane.
c Drying their hair.

10 When was the first ever airplane flight?

a 1903
b 1744
c 1960

Now check your answers.

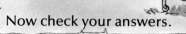

Air alphabet

Pilots use the "phonetic alphabet" to transmit clearly initial letters over the radio. They replace the initials with special words. Flight AS23 becomes "Alpha Sierra two three", for instance. The games on this page use the phonetic alphabet below.

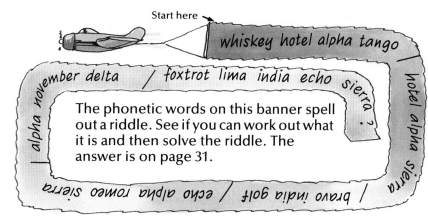

Start here

whiskey hotel alpha tango

alpha november delta / foxtrot lima india echo sierra

hotel alpha sierra

The phonetic words on this banner spell out a riddle. See if you can work out what it is and then solve the riddle. The answer is on page 31.

bravo india golf / echo alpha romeo sierra

A	Alpha	N	November
B	Bravo	O	Oscar
C	Charlie	P	Papa
D	Delta	Q	Quebec
E	Echo	R	Romeo
F	Foxtrot	S	Sierra
G	Golf	T	Tango
H	Hotel	U	Uniform
I	India	V	Victor
J	Juliet	W	Whiskey
K	Kilo	X	X-ray
L	Lima	Y	Yankee
M	Mike	Z	Zebra

Did you know?

When you take off in a plane you get a popping feeling in your ears, because the pressure of the air around you goes down as you leave the ground. To get back to normal suck a hard candy, yawn or swallow.

Air story

There is one word from the phonetic alphabet missing in the story below. Which is it?

It was November in the Sierra. The Hotel Lima was fully booked. During the day many people played golf, and at night the echo of the foxtrot floated up from the dance floor into the air.

Papa Alpha , the head waiter, wore a smart red uniform. One night he organized a fancy dress competition. Mike, from Quebec, went as Romeo, and his wife went as Juliet. Charlie Delta went as a doctor.

But he drank too much whiskey, fell over doing the Tango, and had to go for an x-ray. Oscar from India was the victor, for his zebra outfit. Bravo! he won a kilo of chocolates.

Air race

This air race is for two players. The winner is the first person to get their plane from Fogsville to Cloudsville airport. You need a dice or a scorer (see page 3) and two markers to use as planes. Make one each by writing your name on a small slip of paper. Spread the book out on a flat surface to play.

How to play

1 Park your marker on one of the start squares. Take turns to throw the dice or spin the scorer. Move your plane the number of squares thrown.

2 You must start by flying along the route leading from your start square. Then obey the instructions on the squares you land on.

3 When both planes are on the same route they can overtake each other, but they cannot land on the same square.

4 If you throw a number which lands on the same square as another plane, stay where you are until your next turn.

5 You must land on the same color runway as you started, so you might need to change lanes at the end.

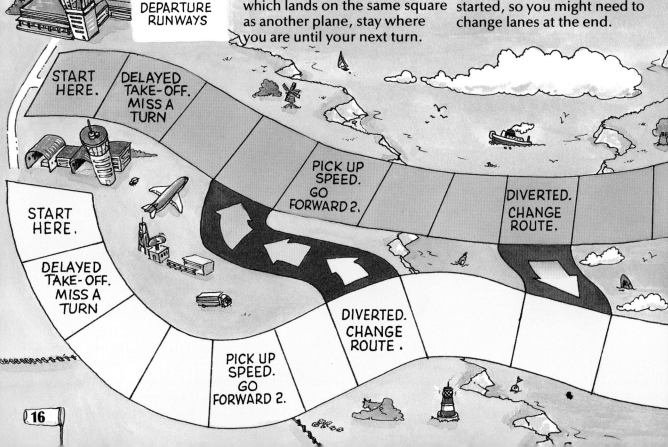

FOGSVILLE DEPARTURE RUNWAYS

START HERE.

DELAYED TAKE-OFF. MISS A TURN

START HERE.

DELAYED TAKE-OFF. MISS A TURN

PICK UP SPEED. GO FORWARD 2.

PICK UP SPEED. GO FORWARD 2.

DIVERTED. CHANGE ROUTE.

DIVERTED. CHANGE ROUTE.

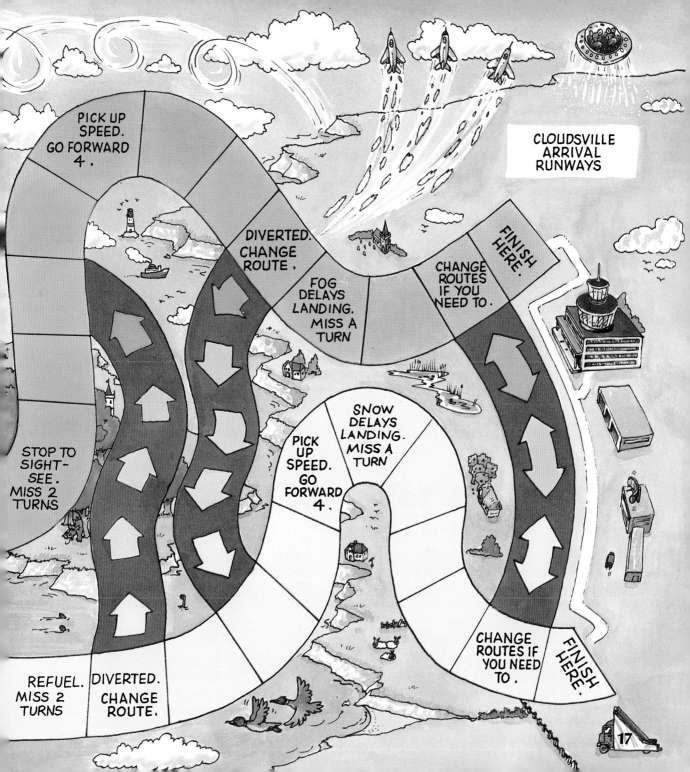

Time changes

The world is divided up into 24 time zones. If you cross a time zone in an airplane you need to move your watch backwards or forwards, depending on the direction you are going in. When it is 1 o'clock in one zone, it is 2 o'clock in the zone to the east of it, and 12 o'clock in the zone to the west of it. See if you can work out the time puzzle on the right.

At 12 o'clock midday it is lunchtime in Fogsville.

Meanwhile, in Suntown people are shopping at 3 pm.

But in Snow City people are waking up at 8 am.

All the towns are marked on this map. Which is which?

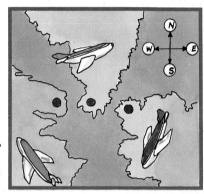

Alphabet row

Try playing this game on board a plane or waiting at an airport. For each passenger you see make up an imaginary name, a job and a place to live, using one letter of the alphabet, beginning at A.

For instance, you could start with Angus Addlebrain, an alligator catcher from Australia and move on to Brenda Boxhead, a brain surgeon from Birmingham, and so on through the alphabet to Z.

Make up the names quietly, so that you don't upset anyone.

"You could include imaginary names, jobs and homes for yourself and your companions in your list!"

Flying fashion

These three flight attendants have got their uniforms all mixed up. See if you can work out who should be wearing what.

Bert

Jim

Mabel

Did you know?

The shortest scheduled flight in the world is between two Scottish islands. It usually takes two minutes but it has been done in a record 58 seconds.

Fill the food tray

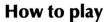

The idea of this game is for you to be a super-efficient flight attendant and collect as many things as you can to fill an airline food tray.

How to play

1 Use a small coin as your marker, or write your name on a small piece of paper.

2 Put your marker at the start and throw a dice or spin a scorer.

3 Move your marker along the row the number of spaces thrown. When you get to the end of a row follow the arrow to move down to the next one.

4 If you land on a space with an object on it, you can collect it for your tray. Make a note of what you collect.

5 If you land on a space which says you can go up or down, you can move to a different row and try to collect any items you have missed.

6 If you get to the end without collecting all the items, try again (start scoring again from the beginning). You could play with a friend to see who collects all the items first.

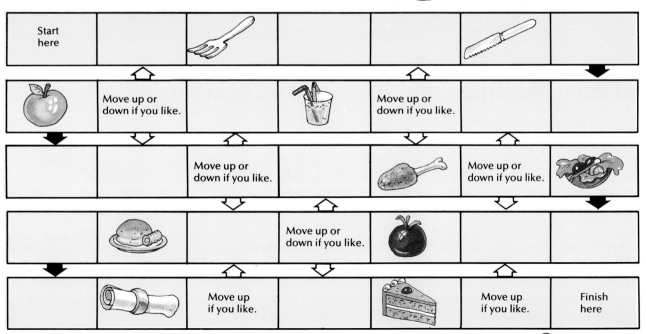

On autopilot

Lou Smyway, Mugsair First Officer, has switched on the autopilot (a machine that flies an aircraft) to guide the Mugsair plane from Fogsville to Costa Fortune. He has programmed the autopilot for a journey including six turns. See if you can work out the route it takes on the map shown on the right.

Fogsville

Costa Fortune

Fancy meeting you

A plane takes off from Fogsville airport on its way to Costa Fortune, 800 km away. Its speed is 350 km per hour. An hour later a plane takes off from Costa Fortune on its way to Fogsville, going at a speed of 400 km per hour.

As the planes pass each other which plane is nearest to Costa Fortune?

Did you know?

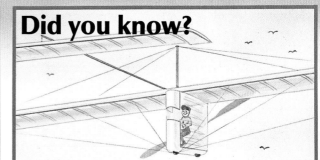

The longest human-powered flight was made in 1979 by a man who pedalled his specially designed craft for two hours and forty-nine minutes between Britain and France. His plane, called Gossamer Albatross, is shown above.

Music mimes

These four passengers are pretending to play the music on their in-flight headphones. See if you can guess which passengers are listening to which records.

RECORD LIST

a "Violin waltz"
b "Trumpet blues"
c "Rockin' drums"
d "Guitar Gertie"

Fit the food

See if you can work out which food tray belongs to which passenger from the clues below.

Ian Trouble wanted ice-cream. He didn't want a hot drink.

Birdman Jack wanted chips, but doesn't like sausages.

D. Racula didn't want ice-cream but did want sausages.

Mrs. Flight wanted a hot drink. She doesn't like chips.

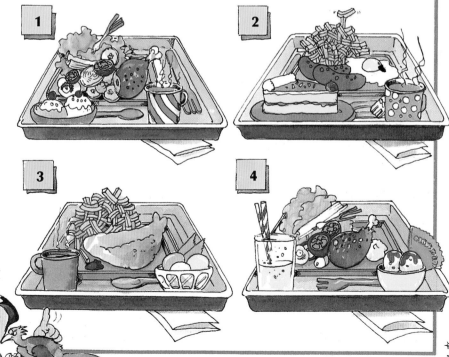

The plane race

START

These veteran planes are lined up for a race to Landingston, 60 km away. See if you can work out in which order they finished and at what time, using the race details below.

Yellow plane

Pilot: **Baron Ripazip**

Take-off time ▶ 3.30 p.m.

20 Speed in km per hour ◀

Refuelling stops 1 10 minutes

Red plane

Pilot: **Roger Andout**

Take-off time ▶ 3 p.m.

15 Speed in km per hour ◀

Refuelling stops 2 10 minutes each

Blue plane

Pilot: **Jock Saway**

Take-off time ▶ 3.15 p.m.

20 Speed in km per hour ◀

Refuelling stops 1 15 minutes

Air acrobatics

This airborne acrobatic team are doing a daring trick. See if you can work out how they made the second pyramid from the first pyramid by moving only three acrobats.

Mixed-up movie

The scenes in this in-flight movie are all mixed up. See if you can work out in which order they should go.

Clear to land

Planes have to line up to land at busy airports by flying in circles at different levels. This is called "stacking". As soon as one plane lands, those above it fly down to the next level in the stack.

The idea of this game is to race with a friend to see who is first to land from one of the stacks below. Choose a stack each, then take it in turns to throw a dice or spin a scorer.

Start with your finger on the top level of your stack. Move down to the next level only when you throw the number shown on the dice beside it.

To play on your own, time how long it takes to move down a stack, then try to beat your best time.

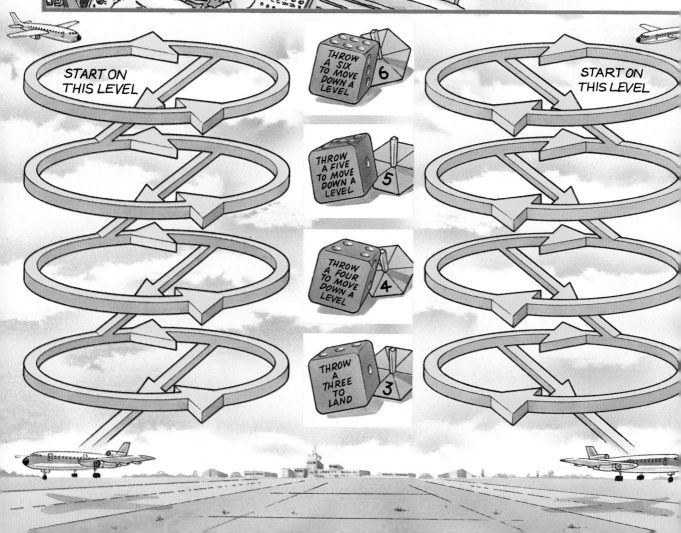

START ON THIS LEVEL

THROW A SIX TO MOVE DOWN A LEVEL — 6

THROW A FIVE TO MOVE DOWN A LEVEL — 5

THROW A FOUR TO MOVE DOWN A LEVEL — 4

THROW A THREE TO LAND — 3

START ON THIS LEVEL

Marshalling maze

Marshals guide planes to parking bays at an airport. They use sticks or batons to make direction signals for pilots to follow. Some of these signals are shown on the right.

MOVE AHEAD   TURN RIGHT   TURN LEFT   STOP!

Follow the Mugsair marshal's signals in the box above to work out which parking bay the plane below is being directed to. Imagine you are the pilot looking out of the front of the aircraft.

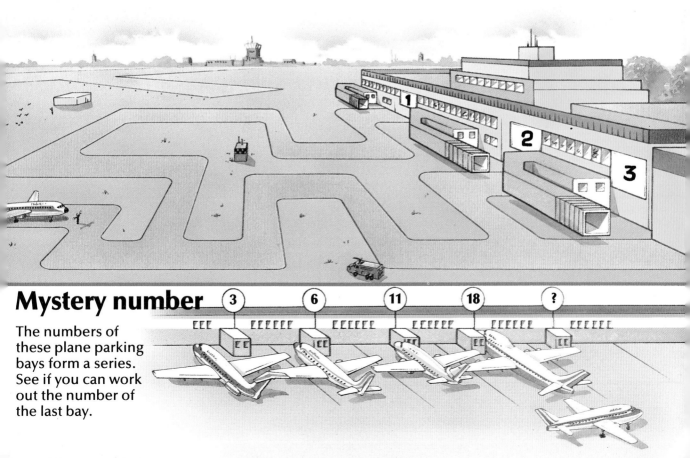

Mystery number

The numbers of these plane parking bays form a series. See if you can work out the number of the last bay.

3   6   11   18   ?

Collect the cases

This is a race for two players, to see who can collect all their baggage first from one of the airport conveyor belts below. Each player needs a small coin to play.

Choose a conveyor belt each. The player on the left must collect all the numbered yellow cases. The player on the right must collect all the numbered red cases. Take turns to throw a dice or spin a scorer and move a coin around your belt the number of squares you have thrown. When you land on a numbered bag you can collect it, by making a note of its number.

The winner is the first person to collect all their baggage.

GO THIS WAY

START HERE. MISS A TURN IF YOU LAND ON THIS SQUARE AGAIN

GO THIS WAY

START HERE. MISS A TURN IF YOU LAND ON THIS SQUARE AGAIN

Map maze

Mrs Flight is studying a map of the departure lounge she is in, to find the Costa Fortune airport exit. See if you can work out which of the three maps below she is looking at.

EXIT

Mrs Flight

1 YOU ARE HERE — EXIT

2 YOU ARE HERE — EXIT

3 YOU ARE HERE — EXIT

Change it

When you go abroad you often need to change your money for the money of another country. Mrs Bagsfull wants to change Fogsville splots for Costa Fortune money so that she can shop at the airport. The table below shows what her splots are worth.

How many splots does Mrs Bagsfull need to change into Costa Fortune money to buy all the things in the shop window below?

Fogsville money		Costa Fortune money
10 splots	=	1 zingo
2 splots	=	1 lug

2 lugs

1 zingo

2½ zingos

4 lugs

Make a superstunt plane

This superstunt paper plane can turn right or left, spin or dive. You can make it from a rectangular-shaped piece of paper by following the steps below. The bigger the paper the bigger your plane will be. To launch the plane, grip it underneath the front and throw it slightly downwards. You could use it at home or outdoors.

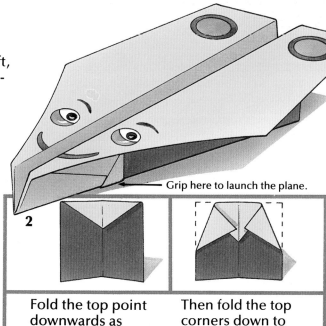

Grip here to launch the plane.

1
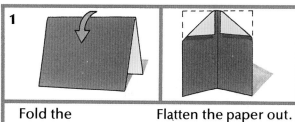

Fold the paper in half lengthways.

Flatten the paper out. Fold the top corners down to the center.

2

Fold the top point downwards as shown above.

Then fold the top corners down to the center fold line.

3
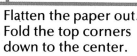

Fold point A up as shown above.

Fold points B and C to the center.

Pinch the center fold together.

4
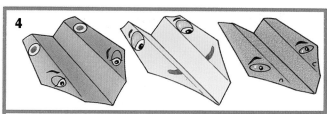

If you like, decorate your plane with colored pens or pencils. You could give it a face and badges on the wings.

Stunt tips

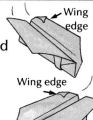

Wing edge

Wing edge

1 Left turn : fold the left wing edge up.

2 Right turn : fold the right wing edge up.

3 Spin : turn the right wing edge up and curve the rudder to the right.

Rudder

4 Dive : fold both the wing edges up.

Did you know?

The record for an outdoor paper plane flight is 2km (1 1/4 miles), set in New York.

Captain's log

Airplane Captains keep a record of their flights in a logbook. You might like to make your own log in a notebook to record the details of your trip. The journey log shown below takes up three pages. It is a good idea to prepare the log beforehand, so you can fill it in as you go along.

You could also make a scrapbook on other pages by sticking in things collected on the journey, like baggage labels or ticket stubs. The pictures below show how to divide the pages of your notebook to make the log.

Page 1 — The departure

Airport name	Fogsville
Date of journey	July 27th
Time of arrival at airport	8.30 a.m.
Gate number	5 (This is where you go to board your plane.)

Page 2 — The airplane

Flight number	321 (This will be marked on your ticket.)
Type of plane	DC10 (Ask a flight attendant.)
Name of airline	Mugsair
Seat number	14 (You will get a boarding pass with a number on it.)

Page 3 — The Flight

Time the flight took	3 hrs. (Time the journey from take-off to landing.)
Where it landed	Costa Fortune (The name of the airport and country.)
Distance travelled	500 splats (Ask a flight attendant.)
What I did on board	Played air travel games

Scrapbook pages

Answers

Page 4
Camera clues
The changes in the camera picture are circled below.

Page 5
Let us out!
The crew push a piece of paper partly under the door. They poke the key out of the keyhole with the end of a spoon, so that it falls onto the piece of paper. Then they pull it back under the door.

Whose jacket?
The Captain has the Flight Engineer's jacket. The First Officer has the Captain's jacket. The Flight Engineer has the First Officer's jacket.

Quick Games
Flight 323 is going to Italy. Flight 297 is going to Greece. Flight 345 is going to Egypt. Flight 595 is going to Russia.

Page 6
Smuggler search
Hans Cuffed is disguised as Ian Flightmovie

Page 6 (continued)
Passport pieces
A and D don't fit Lady Moneybag's picture.

Page 8
Potty's planes
Number 3 is the only plane without wheels.

Air badges
The Gulf Air badge makes up the fourth pair because it shows a winged creature, like the Lufthansa badge. The other pairs also show pictures which are similar.

Sneaky spies
This is the route James Pond took.

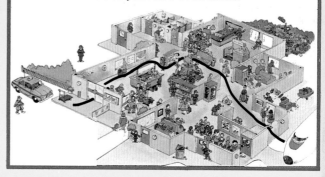

Page 9
Spy catching
The spies are on pages 12, 13, 14, 20 and 27.

Who is it?
Birdman Jack is going to stay with his grandmother.

Page 10
Spot the planes
There is no DC10 at Fogsville, so Peter Perfect's list is the right one.

Page 11
Airport trucks
The scissor platform is missing.

Page 12
Seating plan
James Pond sits in seat 1, Lady Moneybags sits in seat 2, Lotta Trouble sits in seat 3, Peter Perfect sits in seat 4, Rick Ord sits in seat 5 and Mrs Bagsfull sits in seat 6.

A parking problem
Move the planes around in two steps, as shown below.

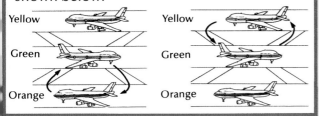

Page 13
Truck mechanic
Hans should mend truck B, because it will take only 50 minutes.

Page 14
The great air quiz
Answers: 1b, 2c, 3a, 4c, 5c, 6b, 7c, 8b, 9a, 10a

Page 15
Air alphabet
Riddle - what has big ears and flies? Answer - a Jumbo.

Air story
The missing word is yankee.

Page 18
Time changes
The towns are shown below.

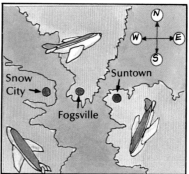

Flying fashion
Jim is wearing Mabel's hat and skirt and Bert's jacket and shoes. Bert is wearing Jim's trousers and hat and Mabel's jacket and shoes. Mabel is wearing Jim's jacket and shoes and Bert's hat and trousers.

Page 20
On autopilot
This is the route the plane takes.

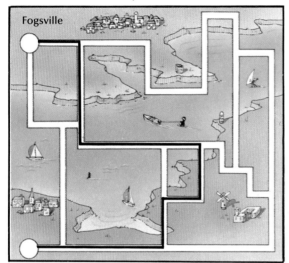

Fancy meeting you
The planes must be the same distance away from Costa Fortune when they pass.

Page 21
Music mimes
Passenger 1 is listening to the Violin Waltz, passenger 2 is listening to Rockin' Drums, passenger 3 is listening to Trumpet Blues and passenger 4 is listening to Guitar Gertie.

Fit the food
Tray 1 belongs to Mrs Flight, tray 2 belongs to D. Racula, tray 3 belongs to Birdman Jack and tray 4 belongs to Ian Trouble.

Page 22
The plane race
The blue plane finishes first at 6.30 p.m., the yellow plane finishes at 6.40 p.m. and the red plane finishes at 7.20 p.m.

Page 23
Air acrobatics
This is how the acrobats made the second pyramid.

Mixed up movie
The correct order of scenes is 5, 1, 4, 3, 6, 2.

Page 25
Marshalling maze
The plane parks at bay 3.

Mystery number
The missing number is 27.

Page 27
Map maze
Mrs Flight is looking at map 3.

Change it
Mrs Bagsfull needs to change 47 splots.

First published in 1986 by Usborne Publishing Ltd, Usborne House, 83-85 Saffron Hill, London EC1N 8RT, England. Copyright © 1986 Usborne Publishing Ltd

American Edition 1986
Printed in Belgium